The Fairy Girls

Do you believe in fairies? If you do, this is the perfect book for you! If you don't, let me convince you that fairies are very magical. Anyways, let's begin the story!

 Once upon a time lived a little girl named Lily. She always loved nature, but she did not fit in with other kids at school. There was something about her that was different, but she never knew what.

On a Thursday morning Lily woke up at 7:00 AM to the sound of her alarm clock. "Lily, breakfast is ready!" her mom called from the kitchen. "Ok mom, I'm coming!" Lily replied. Then they both ate their delicious pancakes. Soon after that, Lily brushed her teeth, brushed her hair, and got dressed into her school uniform. When she was ready, she headed off to the bus station.

When she arrived at school, the popular girls came up to her. One of them named Amanda said: "Everyone come look, the school loser is here!" All of the students gathered around and made rude comments like "Eww, that outfit looks disgusting!" or "What is this loser doing here?" She sat sadly alone at lunch and continued getting bullied throughout the day.

On Friday, Lily's teacher announced that they would be having a new student in class. She was assigned to show the new student around the school. A few minutes later the new student came into the classroom. "Hi, my name is Kate and my favorite color is blue" she said. "Great, now we have another loser in our school" Amanda whispered to one of the other bullies named Maddison, while rolling her eyes. "Everyone, please tell Kate your name and favorite color" the teacher said. All of the students followed the teacher's request. About 30 minutes later, Kate asked, "May I please go to the bathroom?" "Yes you may, Lily will show you the way" the teacher replied. After Lily and Kate left the classroom, Maddison whispered to Amanda: "Finally those nerds are gone". "Yeah, they are so annoying" Amanda whispered back. "Maddison and Amanda, stop talking during class!" the teacher yelled at them.

That day, Lily and Kate became best friends. On the weekend Lily invited Kate to come to her house. "Let's pretend we are sisters!" Kate said. "Yeah, that sounds like fun!" Lily said. They had a sleepover that weekend and it was a lot of fun getting to know each other.

They found out that they had a lot in common; they both loved nature and were different from everyone else they knew. After that day, the two girls always hung out in the forest at recess.

Every time they went to the forest, they kept seeing fairies flying around and they felt strong

connections when they touched plants and insects. It seemed strange at first, but they felt like

they belonged there. As time went by, the girls' connection to nature became stronger and

stronger.

One Wednesday, they went to the same forest during recess as they usually would. As their nature visits became more frequent, the weird connections and feelings intensified. They found two beautiful rocks; one was blue and the other was green (which were their favorite colors). They would have brought the rocks inside, but the teacher did not let any of her students bring anything from recess into the classroom. "Class, recess is over!" the teacher announced that day. At that moment everyone went inside, while the beautiful rocks had to remain in the forest.

After recess they had the P.E. class. "Today we will be outside in three stations," the coach announced loudly. "Station one will have jump ropes, station two will have hula hoops, and the third station will be for free play. The groups today are Lily and Kate, Amanda and Maddison, and the last group is Alex and Zach. Everyone, please pick a station!" All the students ran to their favorite stations and got to work.

Kate and Lily chose the free play station, so that they could go back to the forest and see the beautiful rocks again. As the girls took a closer look, they realized that the rocks they had found were attached to a necklace string. That was a very nice surprise!

"Students, come inside, it's time to go back to your classroom!" the coach called. They all got in a line promptly and walked back to class. As usual, the rocks had to remain outside.

After an hour of class, it was finally lunch time. Both of the mean girls sat next to Lily and Kate. "Let's eavesdrop on their conversation," Maddison whispered to Amanda. "Yeah, that should be a lot of fun" she whispered back. Just then Kate said: "Do you think, Lily, that the necklaces belong to the fairies we saw?" "I don't know, they might," Lily responded. "What are they talking about?" Maddison whispered. "I wonder, where did they see necklaces and fairies???" Amanda said in a soft voice to Maddison. "Tomorrow let's spy on them during recess" Maddison whispered back. "That's a perfect plan"

The next day the mean girls spied on Lily and Kate during recess. "Did you see that fairy?!" Lily asked. "Yeah I did, it was so beautiful" Kate said. "I didn't see anything," Amanda said to Lily and Kate. "Stop pretending you saw one," Maddison said. "We actually did see one with our own two eyes" Kate told them. "They are probably just playing a make believe game" Amanda said. "Yeah, let's get out of here!" Maddison agreed. "Why do you think they were spying on us, don't they want to do something else at recess?" Kate asked. "I don't know, and how did they even find us all the way in the forest?" All of these questions were running through their heads when they suddenly heard a fairy ask: "What are your names?" They were shocked! Was it a real fairy, or just their imagination? "Our names are Lily and Kate," they answered politely. "Ok, I will see you around in this forest!" the fairy said. "That was weird" Lily and Kate said at the exact same time. They wanted to discuss what had happened, but before they knew it, recess was over.

Unable to forget the talking fairy, Lily asked Kate during lunch: "Do you think that was a real fairy!?" "I don't know, but it looked like one! That was super magical, but why couldn't Maddison and Amanda see the fairies?" asked Lily. "I know, right, it's really strange," Kate replied.

The next day, the girls figured out that they were the only ones in the school who could see the fairies. All of the other students said that Lily and Kate were making it up, and that they were wasting their time. Lily and Kate were pretty upset because they didn't understand why other people could not see the fairies. Then, the same fairy from the other day came up to them and said, "Don't worry darlings, you two are very special. It is not a bad thing that no one else can see us; it is actually more of a good thing". At first, the girls didn't believe her and assumed that she was just trying to make them feel better. But just a few seconds later the fairy proved to them that she wasn't lying. She told them that they were the only ones who could play with fairies and have a strong bond with them. As the days went by, Lily and Kate started to become closer with the fairies. They had a lot of fun together, and soon made their own fairy club. As more fairies joined in, the students remained confused.

Although Lily and Kate always thought they were special, they never knew they were *THAT*

special. I mean, they could see *FAIRIES! REAL FAIRIES!!!* They were no longer confused

about their discovery, but they still wondered why no one else could see the fairies. It was very

strange, considering they were just like any other kids. Or were they?

The next whole month was pretty much the same. But then, things started to change. Amanda

and Maddison started to believe Kate and Lily that the fairies were real. You might think that

was a good thing, but it wasn't. The mean girls got jealous that they couldn't play with the

fairies. "That isn't fair!" Maddison said. "Yeah, why can't we play with the fairies?" Amanda

agreed. It wasn't long until they all got into a big fight. Maddison and Amanda pushed Kate and

Lily on the ground; and fairies fought back. Maddison and Amanda said that going to the nurse

was for babies, so Lily and Kate went alone. They got up off the ground and headed off. When

they arrived, the nurse asked, "Hello, what happened to you girls?" "We got into a fight during

recess," Lily said. "Yeah, but it's nothing serious," Kate told her. "Here, take some bandages and two bags of ice," the nurse said as she handed them some supplies. "Thanks nurse" Lily said gratefully. "Happy to help, I hope you feel better soon!" the nurse replied.

When they got back to class, they got a surprise! The fairies were in class! "You guys can sit in those two chairs," the teacher told them. Then the fairies got up and left the room. "Hello, Earth to Kate and Lily?" the teacher asked. "Oh sorry, we will take a seat now" they replied quickly. Later that day during lunch, one of the fairies named Twilight said, "We wanted to make sure that you'd come back to class" "Yeah, we had to see if you were ok" another fairy named Crystal told them. "Thanks, guys!" Lily and Kate said at the same time. Then, they all laughed together.

It was 2:00 pm on the same day, when Crystal and Twilight came to check on Lily and Kate. The fairies said that they signed them up for a doctors appointment so Lily raised her hand and told the teacher, "Me and Kate have to go to a doctors appointment" "Ok, you are excused from class for the day" the teacher said. "What, how is that fair!?" Maddison asked angrily. "Yeah, they are probably lying just so they can get out of class!" Amanda agreed. "They are very good students, they would never lie" the teacher disagreed. Then, Lily, Kate, Twilight, and Crystal headed off for the doctor.

"Hello Dr. Michael," Kate said kindly. "Hello girls," he said. "Someone called in and said that there might be something wrong with you, let me go get some of the tests" Dr. Michael told them. As soon as he left the room Lily yelled to Twilight and Crystal, "Why did you say that there was something wrong with us!?" "Yeah, I thought we were just having a check-up!" Kate agreed. "We have our reasons," Crystal said.

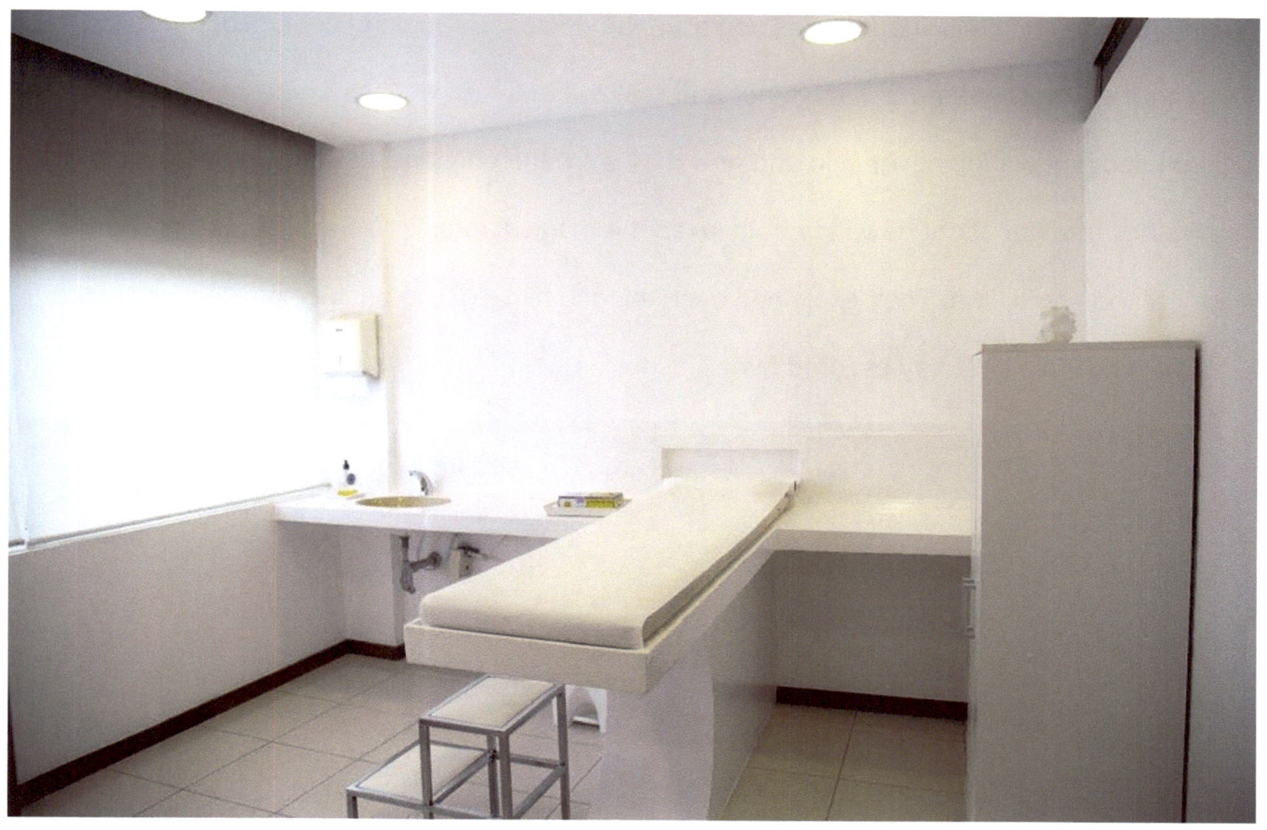

Lily and Kate were suspicious, but they just played along with it. They knew that if they kept asking about it, the fairies would get annoyed and never tell them why they said such a thing. So, they kept quiet. When Dr. Michael entered the room, he was holding a machine. The girls were confused about what this was, but then it hit them. This was the "test" he was talking about.

The girls took the test and soon after got their results. "This is interesting," the doctor told them. "What is interesting?" Lily and Kate both said at the exact same time. "You guys are sisters," he said. "Really!?" Kate said. "Yes but the really interesting thing is that you guys aren't even human, but we can't tell what species you are," the doctor said looking confused.

Then, Lily and Kate looked at each other and realized that they do look pretty similar. They also thought about how they never fit in and how they were the only ones that could see fairies. And finally, they thought about how they both loved the magical forest. "We are fairies!" they told the doctor at the same time. They explained everything to him. "Come back next week for another test," he said. "We will," Lily assured him.

That night, the girls told their parents about what had happened that day. Both of their families gathered for dinner. The moms told Lily and Kate a true story that happened to themselves; One day they were sunbathing on the beach, when a magical portal appeared. Out of that portal came Lily and Kate. They had name tags so both moms knew the names of the children. They also were wearing princess crowns. Kate's family had to move for a business opportunity. After

7 years, they decided it was time for the sisters to meet. So Kate moved schools, and the girls became best friends. They always liked to pretend to be sisters but little did they know they were sisters in real life too.

"I think it is time for you guys to meet your real mom" Kate's dad said. "Me too," said Lily's dad. "We agree," both moms said. "We have done a lot of research and know where the wizard lives," Lily's mom said. "Where does he live?!" The girls said at the same time. "He lives in the forest behind your school," Kate's mom told them. They figured that this was the reason they felt a connection in that forest. So they packed their bags and snuck into the forest at their school. They had to walk for about 30 minutes but they finally reached a small cabin in the woods.

They entered the cabin and saw a wizard with a white beard, purple hat and red cloak. He said, "Hello, what can I help you with?" "We need to go to the fairy forest," Kate said. "Ok, but I need your ticket," he said. "Ticket?" Lily asked. "You need tickets since you are not transformed into fairies yet" the wizard explained, "They are 2000 dollars each" "Where are we supposed to get 2000 dollars!?" the girls said together. "I don't know, but you have to get it if you want to go to the fairy forest" he said. The girls tried to do a bake sale the next day, but they only made 15 dollars. "Girls, we know you really want it, so we decided to put all of our money together to get you 4000 dollars. "Thank you guys so much!" the girls told their adopted parents.

"Bye mom and dad, we will miss you!" the girls said. "We will miss you too," the parents told the girls. Then, they all hugged and off the girls went on their journey. They jumped through a portal and started falling down a big hole. It took a while, but when they reached the bottom, they remembered everything. They ran to the castle, and said hi to the queen. "Oh my gosh, our daughters are back!" she said. The girls were confused, but then it hit them. Their adopted parents said that they were wearing princess crowns. This meant that the queen was their mom!

That night, the queen announced that they were having a dinner feast to celebrate the return of Lily and Kate. Everyone had to wear their best outfit, so the girls got to work. They both had their own fashion designer to help them choose what to wear. They soon picked out their dresses and tried them on. The dresses fit perfectly! Kate's dress was white with blue flowers and Lily's dress was plain dark green, but very long and beautiful.

Both of the girl's dresses were stunning! They just needed one last thing to complete the looks; their princess crowns. They looked all over the castle, but the crowns were nowhere to be seen. A few minutes later, they got a call from their adopted parents. They said that they would mail the princess crowns to them as fast as they could. "Thank you!" the girls said together. 30

minutes later the crowns arrived. They looked very beautiful.

The girls put their crowns on and were ready to go to the royal feast. When they got to the table they saw 2 boys with crowns. Then, Lily and Kate's mom said "Zach, Alex, please introduce yourselves" "I recognize those names" Lily and Kate thought. "We used to go to Mcgreens Elementary School" Zach said. "And we are brothers by the way" Alex told them.

"We used to go to the same school!" Lily and Kate yelled at the same time. "We are Lily and Kate!" They told the boys at the exact same time. "Actually, all 4 of you guys are siblings," their mom said. "*WHAT?!*" they all screamed.

"Yes it's true" their mom told them truthfully. They all sat there for a while thinking about how this makes any sense. They didn't really talk to each other a lot, but Alex and Zach weren't very popular either. They all said at the same time, "It makes sense!!!"

Then, the girls sat down in silence while the cook handed everyone their food. As everyone started eating, their dad (the king) said "Tomorrow we have a celebration that the long lost princesses have arrived" "Yes Father" the kids said. Then, the girls got up and went to their room.

They both took showers, and jumped into some comfy Pajamas. After that, they put their hair in ponytails and layed down to watch TV.

After about an hour of watching TV, their dad announced "Time to start getting ready for bed!"

They all switched the TV off and pulled the covers over themselves.

The next morning they woke up to a very fancy breakfast on their bedside table. This breakfast

was way fancier than some pancakes that they used to have every morning.

They got some beautiful royalberry cinnamon rolls with some sweet tea for a beverage. They all

ate up and got dressed.

The whole day, they thought about the differences between Fairy Forest and the human world:

in the human world, they always had pancakes for breakfast, while in the Fairy Forest, they had a royal feast. Also, in the human world they were the shy nerds, and in Fairy Forest, they are

part of royalty.

Although they were treated a lot worse, they missed the human world. All 4 children. That same

day, the siblings decided to show the mean girls who's boss! Their parents agreed to come, and

soon after they had left for this adventure.

"Mom, where are we going?" Alex asked. "If we want to go back to the human world, we will

have to get a potion from the wizard", their mom replied. "Dad, can we stop for a snack?" the

siblings said at the exact same time. Everyone bursted into laughter. After the laughing was

done, their dad said, "Good thing I brought my backpack!" They all sat on a nearby bench and

ate up.

Once they were full, they continued with the journey. It took about half an hour, but they

eventually made it to the wizard's house. "Hello, may I help you guys?" the wizard asked. "We

need a potion to make us visible to humans, and we also want to go through the portal back to

the human world" Kate said. "Ok" he said, "You guys can get it for free because you are royalty"

"Ok, thank you sir", said Zach. "Drink these while you are in the portal", the wizard told them as

he handed each of them a potion. "Let's do this!" Lily shouted. They all jumped through the

portal at the same time while drinking the potions.

They got to the human world, went to their old school, and met the mean girls at recess, they

showed Amanda and Maddison that they weren't playing a game at all and that they truly are

fairies. After they all finished talking, the mean girls got upset so they told the teacher to come

over there, but before the teacher could get there the fairies had already vanished.

They left the human world to go back to Fairy Forest. After that day they lived happily ever after

as a royal fairy family.

The   End